M. Romance

LIFE BEFORE DAMAGED
VOLUME 8

THE FERRO FAMILY

BY:

H.M. WARD

LAREE BAILEY PRESS

www.SexyAwesomeBooks.com

COPYRIGHT

LAREE BAILEY PRESS
First Edition: August 2015
ISBN: 9781630350826

LIFE BEFORE DAMAGED

Volume 8

WHEN RADIOACTIVE SAUSAGES CAN FLY
October 19th, 2:56pm

"I'm going to be sick." I try to swallow but my heart is in the way. It's stuck in my throat, and has been there since we took off.

"You're not going to be sick."

The pitch of my voice rises as I ramble, "Are you sure this is safe? The plane is too little. I mean, look at it. I can reach the tip of the wing from here." I can't, not really, but it's so tiny. "It can't possibly be safe to have so many people shoved in a shoebox with wings. We're sitting on the floor for crying out loud! What if we're too heavy? I saw that guy looking at us before he took some of the gas off the plane. What if we crash?"

The plane shudders and I tense before leaning into Philip a little bit more. He's sitting behind me with his legs on either side of mine, his arms wrapped around my waist. I feel him chuckle, before dropping a kiss on my head.

My stomach is close to jumping out of my mouth. Where are the puke baggies?

"Relax, Gina. The plane won't break. Trust me. Even if it did, we're already wearing parachutes. We couldn't be safer."

Philip's fingers gently push my ponytail to the side, and he nuzzles my neck. He's doing his best to reassure me, but it's not working.

"Uh, no. You all have parachutes strapped to your backs. I don't. I only have a harness, remember? No parachute for Gina! Gina just gets this neon pink jumpsuit. I look like a radioactive sausage and everyone knows what happens to those!"

In contrast, Philip looks like a freaking model. His sleek black jumpsuit clings to his toned form and accentuates just how fit he really is. Bright red rolls lining his arms serve as handles for other skydivers to grab onto when they do free fall group formations. The thought makes my stomach roll. I rest the back of my head on his hard chest and close my eyes.

"It's okay."

I swallow hard and peel my eyes open. "Why did I agree to do this?"

"Because you love the rush just as much as I do? Because your schoolwork is wearing you down?"

"Oh yeah, right, school."

That's the lame excuse I gave him to explain the funk I've been in since my last meeting with Pete. I still can't force myself to tell him the truth.

The past month has gone by so fast. I've spent most of my time studying and going to wild parties at the swing club. It's been amazing.

As an added bonus--or complication--Philip and his group of skydiving buddies started hanging out at Ricky's club. It's become their turf. I try to keep my distance, but I like him--a lot--and resisting him is becoming harder and harder.

Philip is a gentleman, never pushing for more than stolen kisses and gentle touches, but I can tell he wants more. Part of me wants that, too. It's flattering to be with someone who wants me and only me, someone whose eyes never wander. But a bigger part of me is still hesitant.

It's becoming increasingly difficult to find excuses for why I can't invite him up to my apartment or why I can't go back to his place. The truth is I need to come clean with him about my future engagement to Pete before I can go to bed with him.

Philip is a good man with honest values. He deserves a devoted girlfriend, someone available to one day share his name. A relationship with me would reduce him to be the illicit lover of another man's wife. My fate is fixed while his is fluid.

Philip should be the center of a woman's universe--not her side dish.

I hate holding back the truth from him, but Constance is already angry with me. My new 40's pinup look doesn't jive with the wholesome, good girl image I used to have, and it's pissing her off. If she discovered I told someone outside our families about her little blackmailing scheme, I'm pretty sure she'd skin me and throw my hide on her boardroom floor.

Then there's Pete.

My failure to rein in her son has her seething even more.

Peter Ferro.

My heart clenches at the thought of him. The tabloids claim he's been whoring it up again, spending insane amounts of money on extravagant parties, and getting into fights at every turn. I'm worried about him. I search each photo of him and have yet to see life in his eyes. It's like the vampire whores sucked it away, along with other things. But I know it's more than that.

Part of me suspects that I might be the reason for his behavior; like he's trying to prove me wrong.

"Hey, look at me." Philip cups my chin with his hand and turns my head towards him, breaking me out of my daydreams. "It's normal to be nervous your first time jumping. I promise that it's safe. In fact, skydiving is safer than riding in a car. Believe me, I've done hundreds of jumps already. Just relax, okay?"

I nod, pretending once more that the cause of my mood is something other than concern for my future husband.

Zeke, one of Philip's skydiving buddies and one of my least favorite people, sits across from us and is quick to pick up on my fragile state. "Don't worry, babe. Fatal accidents only happen every 200 jumps or so, and we haven't had one in, let me think... 199 jumps." He shrugs his shoulders and clucks his cheek. "Aw, shit! Sorry, babe. I guess your time is up. Sucks to be you. Speaking of sucking, how about a quickie before you go?" He starts to unzip his jumpsuit in front of everyone.

"Doucheface." I glare at him.

"Back off, Zeke." Philip kicks his friend in the shins.

"What the fuck, man? Whatever happened to 'sharing is caring?' Oh, that reminds me, dude, don't forget that we have a meeting later." Zeke looks me up and down with creepy slithering eyes. "You gonna bring this pretty piece of ass with you?"

Philip tightens his hold around my waist, pulling

me close to him. I can feel the tension rolling off of him. "I said to back the fuck off, Zeke."

I've never heard Philip use such a menacing tone before, which makes the freaky vibe wafting off of his friend even worse. I cuddle into Philip's arms more, putting as much distance between me and Zeke as possible. He stands and turns toward the back of the plane, laughing under his breath.

"Don't listen to that asshole," Philip whispers into my ear. "His mother never loved him as a child."

I try to forget about Zeke, but the plane is small and his eyes lock on mine from the back of the plane. Thankfully, we've reached our desired altitude and everyone is distracted checking on each other's equipment.

It's time. The butterflies in my stomach swarm and fly out my nose. I can't breathe.

One skydiver opens the door of the plane and I shriek, even though I knew it would happen. Everyone looks at me.

I clamp my hand over my mouth and feel my face burning up. Classic Gina.

Over everybody's laughter, I hear Zeke's voice mutter, "Newb."

I don't want to be a human pancake who ends up in Pinelawn.

Phillip walks up to me and takes my hand, giving it a reassuring squeeze before checking our security devices. My instructor does the same with Phillip's gear. When everything is triple checked, Philip cups my face in his hands, coaxing me to lift my gaze up to his.

"See you down on the ground. First time's always the best, kind of like losing your virginity. I just wish I could be there with you when it happens. Maybe later you and I can have a shared first of our own? Celebrate, just the two of us?" His thumbs brush my cheekbones gently as he searches my eyes for an answer I can't give him. He doesn't push. Instead, he bends down and kisses me gently before heading toward the door to the plane.

Since I'm doing a tandem dive, my instructor and I are the last ones to jump out, which means I get to see everyone else jump out of the plane. Philip and his friends slowly make their way to the door, going over last second instructions on the formations they'll be doing during their free fall. One by one they step out and get sucked away in a rush of air.

I feel my instructor laughing behind me, but my heart isn't laughing. It's cowering somewhere inside my stomach, bracing against a lethal impact.

My teacher person tugs on the straps of our parachutes, securing my back tight against his front. We clumsily walk toward the door to the plane, where I look down.

Crap. I shouldn't have done that. Thirteen

thousand feet of frigid nothingness blows in my face. I lower my goggles and allow my instructor to guide me into the proper exit position: arms crossed, gloved hands gripping opposite shoulders, knees bent, feet dangling. The only thing keeping me in the plane is my harness fastened to his. He holds onto the door frame and, with a push and pull, we somersault into the air.

Everything spins rapidly and, for a fraction of a second, I see the underside of our airplane.

FREAKY CHEEKY JAM AND TONSIL EXAM
October 19th, 3:17pm

We toss, turn and tumble wildly in the air. I don't know which way is up or down; everything is going by so fast. The rush of air in my ears is deafening. A scream tries to escape my throat but can't. Breathing is difficult in this wind, making screaming impossible.

After what seems like an eternity, I feel a tap on my shoulder. It's the signal. I lift my arms out to my sides, my elbows bent. We stabilize, and it no longer feels like we're falling. It's more like we're suspended in space, being pushed up by tremendous gusts of wind. The instructor gives me a thumbs up. Since we can't hear each other over the wind, this is his way of asking if I'm ok. I respond by showing him a thumbs up, and we continue our fall.

My cheeks are flapping in the wind and I'm thankful I didn't ask for the video of Gina's freaky cheeky jam and tonsil exam.

My heart is still up in the plane, and I'm waiting for it to catch up with us. A part of me starts freaking out. We're supposed to free fall for about a minute before the chute is supposed to open. It feels like five minutes, not one.

Has my instructor passed out?

Are the security devices not working?

Is our main chute broken?

Is our safety chute defective, too?

Oh, shit! I'm going to die! Why do I keep doing stupid stuff like this?

I'm jostled from a horizontal to a vertical position by a painless tug on every strap of my harness and then... silence and calm. The chute opens, the wind dies down, and it's easier to breathe. We're gently floating.

Breathless, I stare down at the world below.

That was...

That was...

Oh, my GOD! I'm flying! I let out a high pitched squee and kick my feet back and forth.

My instructor navigates as we slowly descend

under our canopy. Everything slows, and I can appreciate the view. Long Island is breathtaking, its thickets of green leaves contrasting against the pale sand and vast expanse of surrounding water. It's so peaceful up here.

Suddenly, the canopy dips and we end up on our side, spinning around in circles. We're gaining speed.

I'm about to grip onto my instructor's arm--something we were specifically told not to do--when the canopy straightens itself again. We're back in a vertical position, floating peacefully once more. Instructor Man shoots another thumbs up sign from behind me and I burst out laughing.

Oh, my God! He did it on purpose!

The guy wiggles his thumbs up in front of my face again waiting for my reply. Giddy, I put up two thumbs and have them dancing around in front of us. The vibrations of his chest against my back tell me that he's laughing at my reaction. I barely have time to catch my breath before he tilts us the other way. We go back into a tailspin, spinning wildly, longer and faster than the last time. I smile so broadly I think my cheeks will crack. The rush is amazing. It's like I'm stuck in a never-ending squee.

After another couple of minutes, the buildings below slowly come into focus. A strange feeling of sadness takes over as I realize my short time in the air, my time away from all of my worries, is almost over.

The closer we get to the ground, I'm able to identify smaller shapes. I see cars in the parking lot, people walking from the landing field to the drop zone office carrying unpacked chutes in their arms, people enjoying drinks on the terrace outside.

Along the edge of the landing field, someone dressed in black clothing leans against a sporty black motorcycle. I'd recognize that silhouette anywhere. It's Pete.

BETTER THAN SEX
October 19th, 3:25pm

I'm accustomed to being followed by Ferro staff everywhere I go. It's not a complete surprise to see someone from their clan waiting for me, but it's never Pete. I haven't seen him since his night with the stripper. That night saddens me. I don't understand him. I thought I did, but I don't.

As the ground gets closer and closer, I bend my knees, making sure my feet aren't in the instructor's way while we land. With our shoes safely on the ground, he unhooks my harness from his own and sends me off to celebrate while he gathers the parachute.

Adrenaline courses through my veins, making my body vibrate deliciously. I walk towards Pete with a big ass smile plastered across my face. He steps toward me, away from his bike. He's frowning, arms folded tightly across his chest.

Ignoring the sinking feeling in my stomach, I jog towards him while jabbing my finger up to the sky, still totally high on adrenaline. I shout to him since he's still a few steps away, "Oh, my God! Did you see that?" I whirl around laughing, lifting my head toward the sky.

Pete's stance relaxes as I approach him; he drops his arms to his sides and smiles. Those blue eyes are watching me. They flick between my open hands to the smile on my lips, before resting on my face. I probably look like a Muppet on Pixie Sticks.

"I jumped out of a plane! A PLANE!" I shove my thumb into my chest and smile so big that it feels like my face won't be able to handle the massive wattage. "GINA JUMPED!" Giggling, I spin around, arms open, swinging freely through the air.

Pete doesn't move toward me. He remains where he is, and it's as if he wants me to be happy. In that moment, he sees me and accepts me—dork and all. Because I'm sure I look a little scary with a ponytail that was chewed by rats and then electrocuted. It's still sticking out even after I stop spinning.

Our eyes meet and life pauses for a second. My

heart is pounding in my chest and I feel free. I wish I could feel that way with him—with Pete. I wish for so many things at once that there are no words to accompany the thoughts. It's a rush of emotions and dreams, and Pete Ferro is in them, and I don't mind.

The corner of his mouth tugs up into a crooked smirk. He takes a deep breath, filling his chest and making that dark t-shirt cling even tighter to his ripped body. The wind blows his hair forward, across his forehead, making it look like sex hair—the kind that's a total mess, and very alluring.

Before I can stop myself, I feel the corner of my mouth pull up. I'm mirroring that crooked smile and holding his gaze. The rush running through me becomes laced with hope.

I should be scared. He shouldn't be here, but I'm not letting what-if's rule me, not anymore. I'm happy, for once, I'm in the best mood of my life and I did this. I jumped.

I stop thinking. I need to be who I want and this girl wants to jump up and down with her friend. My gaze shifts to Pete's hands and I take off at a run. I throw myself at him, wrapping my arms around his neck. He spins me around once and puts my feet gently back down on the ground. His eyes sparkle with joy I haven't seen in a long time.

I glance up at the sky and laugh before I start spewing out words faster than I can form thoughts. "That was, that was... holy fuck—that was better than sex!"

Pete grins, his eyes wide, and rubs his hand over his jaw. "Better than sex?"

When I realize what I said, my cheeks start to burn. A funny smile forms on my face and I avert my eyes to the ground. "I stand by my statement." I shrug one shoulder and giggle to cover up how squirmy I feel inside.

Pete's still holding me, his arms around my waist. He's towering over me, with those smoldering eyes and sexy lips turned up with a teasing grin. "Then, you're doing it wrong, or your partner is utterly lacking." He taps the tip of my nose with one finger.

My chest expands as I try to catch my breath, but it's as pointless as trying to breathe during freefall. If sex with Pete is better than skydiving, I can't survive that level of intensity. There's no way.

My lips quirk up into a coy smile. "There is no way that falling from the sky gives less of a rush than..."

He leans in so close to my ear that I can feel his warm breath on my neck. "Falling for me? Go ahead and ask."

I suck in air and feel my back go ram-rod straight. I'm way too aware of my boobs in my hot pink jumpsuit. It's like his eyes are hands and they're tracing me slowly, teasingly. This is just the way he likes to play. He's all flirt and fiction. Laughing, I lean in and press my lips to his ear. "You're a little too full of yourself, Mr. Ferro. I think someone needs to take you down a notch and tell you no once in a while, so let me help you out—there is no way sex with you is better than this."

As I speak my eyelashes flutter against his cheek. Pete is very still, barely breathing, and when I pull away, his eyes are sharply focused on my mouth. His jaw is tight as if he were trying not to take the bait and refute me. It's like he wants to say something but can't—or won't.

My brows come together as my gaze narrows. "Well, this is a surprise. The sex king bites his tongue and fails to reply. Just remember that you had more than one occasion to put out, and you chose to say no. So, you don't get any of this." I gesture to my curves and arch my back forcing out my S-curve. It was meant to be silly. I look like a lunatic, but Pete's lips part and he stares at me.

That look makes my heart pound for all the wrong reasons. Butterflies are forming inside of me and I don't like this. It's hard because this version of Pete is the one he hides from everyone, but it's the one I see. It's the Pete who rarely shows his face. He's sincere, funny, warm, and caring—his gaze could make a gaggle of girls orgasm simultaneously. Suddenly, heat envelopes me and I need to put space between us. I step back and catch my breath.

Pete is too quiet. My pulse hammers in my ears

and this feeling of wanting more than just his friendship—wanting him to accept who he really is—wanting him to want me, frightens me. He fucks everyone, but he pushed me away. I should hate him. I want to, but then this happens and I feel drawn to him. There's more there, there's a man beneath the surface and he's drowning, trying so hard to escape.

I understand. I know that feeling all too well.

Crap. I look back up to the sky, at the multitude of rainbow colored canopies floating down toward the open landing field. I desperately want to run. I can't stand this. I can't tolerate his feelings because he reminds me of myself. I wasted my life and missed out on amazing things because I was too scared.

Fuck that.

Pete still has a serene, pensive look on his face. Smiling, I dart toward him intending to press a quick kiss to his lips, but he pulls away. My head lunges forward and my mouth connects with nothing. Pete's hands are on my shoulders holding me back.

Rejection? Really? Swallowing hard, I step back and shake out of his grip. "Nice to see you, Ferro. If you'll excuse me, I need to go sign up for another jump." I spin on my heel and intend to jog off, but he reaches for me.

Pete puts a firm hand on my arm just above my elbow, stopping me and pulling me back toward him. "Gina, wait."

I refuse to meet his gaze. I look everywhere, but at his face. My smile is too big and my voice is too chipper. I want him to let go and stop touching me, but I don't want to rip my arm away. I don't want him to know that he hurt me.

Laughing lightly, I cock my head to the side. "It's better than sex, remember? I'm going for multiple orgasms here. After all, a girl has to take care of her own pink parts anyway. It's not an everyday thing where I can get all, *oh baby please.*" When I say those three words, I'm joking. I close my eyes, lean my head back, and expose my neck. I touch my fingers to my throat lightly and trail my hand down along my breast as I speak breathlessly. Loudly. I beg and gasp before sucking in a ragged breath.

When I jerk my head upright and glance toward the desk, wondering if I have time to take another dive, I happen to glance at Pete in the process.

His eyes are wide and the centers have turned to deep pools. Longing is etched on his face and he positions his lips as if something stole his breath— and his heart. The tension in his arms are gone and he seems to be leaning toward me, as if there's something pulling him toward me.

Irritated I huff, "Oh, what the hell? I was kidding, Ferro. Get over yourself! Go find a hose and cool off."

I take off again, and Pete snaps out of it.

His voice is strange, weak. "Gina, wait." He steps toward me and pulls me back.

My eyes drop to the hand holding onto my arm, then up to his face. "What?"

His expression is wavering, flipping between coy and serious. "Although I'm always in favor of multiple orgasms, that's not in the cards for you today--at least not here. My mother sent me to retrieve you."

My chin extends forward as my eyes widen. "Excuse me?"

"You're moving into the house as of now, and there's no choice this time. She won't take no for an answer. Your things have already been moved."

BREAKING UP SUCKS MONKEY BALLS

October 19th, 3:41pm

"WHAT!? How? Why?"

"Isn't it obvious? You've become unpredictable, and she doesn't like unpredictable. She wants you close to keep tabs on you."

Making an aggravated noise in the back of my throat, I tug on my hair and resist the urge to scream in his face. My voice goes the other way, and becomes sharp and quiet. "I've finally figured out how to deal with this, and this is how she reacts? I still have two and half months before things go to Hell. She can't take them away from me! Dammit,

Pete! This isn't fair, and you know it!"

I scream out in frustration, pulling my hair from its low ponytail, and stomping one foot.

"So, life with me is Hell, huh? Gee, thanks," Pete says in a voice more sad than angry. He lets out a rush of air and shakes his head. Deep blue orbs filled with regret bore holes into me. "I wish there was something I could do but--" Pete looks over my shoulder, and his scowl deepens.

I follow his gaze to see Philip running across the grassy field toward us. I toss my arms up in the air. "How am I supposed to explain to Philip that I'm moving in with you? I thought I had two months, Pete. I need more time."

Pete doesn't get to answer. Philip reaches us and wraps an arm around my shoulders, pulling me close to his body and dropping a kiss on the top of my head. Every instinct I have screams for me to move away from Philip, but I don't.

I can't.

"Hey, Gina! I was looking for you. Is everything okay? How did the jump go?" He nods towards Pete. "Ferro." He says as a polite, man-to-man greeting. Pete nods back, his eyes never leaving mine. "Am I interrupting something?" Philip asks cautiously.

Pete backs up a step, never breaking eye contact with me. "I'll give you two a couple of minutes. I'll be on my bike when you're ready to go."

Pete's eyes flick between Philip and me, pausing on his arm draped over my shoulders. I feel guilty for allowing Philip to touch me at all, and desperately want him to stop. Pete's eyes settle back on me, an apologetic look on his face. "I'm really sorry about this, Gina," he says before turning to walk back to his bike, head slumped and hands in his pockets.

Philip's arm slides off of my shoulders, and he moves between me and Pete. "What was that about? Are you leaving? With Ferro? What's going on, Gina?"

My legs are too tired to hold me up. With the adrenaline rush of the dive wearing off, Pete's bomb and what I have to say to Philip, I can no longer stand. I sit down on the grassy field, legs crossed. I pat the spot next to me.

Philip sits down, but I can tell he's wary. He's a smart man. He can tell something is wrong. I never thought I would break a heart. The feeling disgusts me. I remove my gloves and brush my fingers against the tops of the cool blades of grass.

I want to start with 'I really like you' or 'it's not you, it's me' but that sounds lame. No matter how I try to start, what I have to say sounds like the dumbest thing ever. I have to take the dive. I have no choice. Philip has earned the truth.

"This is going to sound really bad, but I'd rather you hear it from me instead of the tabloids. You remember that Granz Textiles recently merged into Ferro Corp?" Philip nods, waiting. "Part of that merger involves me and Pete. We'll be engaged this winter sometime. He just came to inform me that I have to move into his family's home. Today."

Philip remains silent for a while. My fingers play with the blades of grass, ripping them lengthwise into tiny narrow strips. His silence is long and heavy. If it weren't for the fact that I can still see his legs from the corner of my eyes, I'd think he wasn't here. Finally, he responds in a controlled tone. "I see. You've known this for how long, now?"

Oh, God. He's going to hate me for this. "Since right before Ricky's party." I swallow hard and brace myself for the worst.

Philip pushes off the ground and paces back and forth in front of me. When he stops, he turns and looks down to meet my gaze. His expression is hurt and angry, his voice is loud and agitated as he speaks.

"What am I to you, Gina? Some game? A last fling? I'll tell you what you were to me--a woman I could settle down with, a woman I could build a life with. Now, you tell me you're marrying someone else! And that someone else is a Ferro? I can't compete with that."

He rubs a hand over his face in frustration, then continues, his voice lower, calmer. "I thought you were hesitant to go further with me because you were still getting over your asshole ex-boyfriend. Shows what a schmuck I am. If you had told me sooner you were only in this for a meaningless fuck, I would have been all over that. But now it's too late. There's no way in Hell Ferro will let me touch his girl once you're under his roof. Whatever this is," he motions between us, "has got to be over. He's sent people to the ER for less."

I flinch, remembering the night Pete and I met, the reason we're in this impossible situation in the first place. "Philip, please, I've been doing my best not to cross lines, but it's complicated--I really do like you. I really want to be with you. I enjoy the time we spend together. If things could be different—"

"Different? How? As in me becoming your paramour? Your secret love affair? I'm sorry, Gina, but there's no way I'd want to share you--with any man, for any reason. I'm not wired that way. It's an all or nothing kind of thing. Since you're already his, that makes us nothing." He stands in front of me and shakes his head, looking beyond me, toward where Pete waits for me.

"Philip, please! I'm not his. You see the way he is with other women. Our marriage isn't going to be based on love. It's just an unpleasant stipulation of a business merger and, for reasons I can't explain, I can't back out of it. I wish I could choose you, I just can't."

Philip is quiet for a moment. He looks at his hands and then back at my face. "Gina, I see the way you look at each other. There's more to this than you're telling me, but I'm not interested in hearing about it—not after your treating me like this. I don't want to be friends. I don't want to keep in touch. Have a nice life, Future Mrs. Ferro."

FIRE, ICE, BLOOD, AND SWEAT

November 2nd, 2:43am

Smoke.

My nose crinkles at the acrid odor. I try to breathe through my mouth instead, but the smell of scorching fumes makes my throat seize up.

Fire.

I open my eyes, panicked, sitting up in my new bed, in my new room in Ferro Mansion, drenched in cold sweat. Flames are everywhere, surrounding me. I'm trapped.

I gasp, try to scream but I can't speak. I'm calling for help, but I have no voice. I'm alone, and no one can save me. Terror rips through my body as I press myself into a corner of the room.

Slowly, the flames morph into human shapes. Burning people reach out with flaming arms to pull me into the inferno with them.

I frantically back up on my bed until I'm pressed up against the intricate hardwood headboard, and I scream again. Sizzling hands grasp and pull at me, my skin blisters under their touch. I scan the room with my eyes, desperate for an escape. A clear, narrow path, leads from my bed to the door, but the suite is big.

I have to run. It's the only way out.

I sprint from the bed, blazing hands grabbing at my bare legs as I run. I'm faster; I can do this. I'm not weak anymore, and I break free. I pass the living room and make it to the grand foyer by the wooden front door. I place my hands on the handle and realize the metal is freezing cold. I yank my blistered hand back and glance behind me.

The fiery mob is closing in on me, their faces morphing into focus. It's Philip, Zeke, and their skydiving buddies. They're calling my name, leering, asking me to join them. Philip's normally kind eyes are full of vengeance.

Wrapping my hand with the hem of my nightshirt, I try the handle once more. The door opens, and I run out, expecting to be on the front lawn, but I'm not. I must have gone through the wrong door because there are hallways that stretch endlessly in either direction.

Ice covers the walls. It's so cold. My breath comes out in white puffs of steam, and I hold my arms tightly around me to keep warm. I don't know where to go. Nothing looks familiar anymore.

I turn to my left and run, barefoot. With a stitch in my side, I tear down an endless icy corridor for what seems like hours. Impenetrable ice covers all the doors. I keep sprinting. I finally see the end of the hall. A single, ice-free door faces me. I try the handle. It's neither hot nor cold to the touch, so I turn it.

I'm suddenly outside, on the vast grounds of Ferro Mansion, standing on soft green grass. I'm safe. I bend over at the waist, my hands resting on my knees, trying to catch my breath. I hear laughter from behind a nearby rose bush and tiptoe towards the sound. I wish I hadn't.

On the other side of the bush, Pete sits on his bike, shirtless. Moonlight glistens off of the sweaty sheen on his skin, defining each toned muscle. He's holding a single rose in his hands, caressing the petals gently with his fingers as if it's the most precious thing he owns. Women surround him, dozens of naked women. They are clawing at him, trying to get him off of his bike. He looks at them lustily, hunger in his eyes.

When he sees me, his expression changes. He

appears sad, lost. I step toward him, but the naked women push me back, hissing, their snakelike tongues darting out. Pete drops the rose to the ground, and it freezes on contact, shattering. He kicks the bike's engine to life and takes off, fast. He speeds on the icy covered ground and as he rounds the corner by the front gate, I see the back wheel lose traction.

The motorcycle tire slides out from under him as the bike races forward, and thrusts him into the pavement. His battered body slides toward the front gate, not slowing. Rungs of metal from the ornate decoration at the foot of the gate are shaped like arrowheads. There's no helmet to protect his face, no jacket to save his skin. I scream out as loud as I can, horrified.

My voice fills my head as the cry of terror rips from my body.

Darting up in bed, I gasp. My voice is still in my ears. I must have yelled. My heart is still pounding and my body is covered in sweat. It seemed so real. Even though I know it wasn't, even though everything is fine, my emotions can't recognize the difference. My body is still ready to run or fight.

I push away the damp hair that clings to my face. There's no fire--there never is. I take in my new and now slightly familiar surroundings, taking deep calming breaths. I'm safe. I pick up one of the plush pillows and hug it tightly to my chest.

I've been living in Ferro Mansion for two weeks. My life here isn't so bad if you like cold and loveless isolation. I haven't spoken to Philip since our horrible breakup at the drop zone. Erin tried to stop by several times, but the butler keeps sending her away. All I can get from her are text messages. I miss her.

Pete is kind to me, but I hardly ever see him. Jonathan hangs around the house, but he's a massive flirt--his resemblance to Pete makes me uncomfortable.

I avoid the indoor pool and spa because that seems to be where Mr. Ferro keeps his bouncy boobs. I have no inclination to engage in brain-numbing conversations with them. If I have to listen to the virtues of acrylic, gel, and silk nails again, I'm jumping out of a window.

I feel like I'm in prison, which is fitting, considering that's where I belong. The only locations the Ferro family chauffeurs are allowed to drive me are to school and back. I'm getting a serious case of cabin fever despite the fact that this place is huge and has everything I need--everything except what counts most in a home.

The clock on my nightstand shows 2:58 a.m., and I can't go back to sleep. Pushing the blankets away with my feet, I swing my legs over the side of the bed. I pad across the large room and open the closet door. I step inside and grab my dance bag from the little golden chaise, and pull the strap across my shoulder.

Silently, I pad down the hallways. The only thing that brings me any joy is the unused ballroom I discovered on my second day here. It's my salvation. When I'm not in school or studying in my room, I'm in the ballroom dancing. I dance until I can no longer stand. I dance until I can't feel anything but pain from pointe, or overused muscles crying out for rest.

At least I can fathom that type of pain. I can ice it and make it go away. I wish I knew how to ice the nightmares.

I pad inside and flip on one of the chandeliers. I mute the light so it's glowing softly, only illuminating the center of the room ever so slightly. Mirrors surround the edges at various places as does ornate gold moldings. The combination of gold and pale light makes it feel like candles glowing around me.

There's a scent in this room too, something fresh and free. It's somewhere between lilacs and rain showers. It's a happy scent, something from childhood that I can't quite put my finger on. The ceiling is like a canvas, painted by a master. It's not a copy of the Sistine Chapel or something that existed long ago, but rather, it's something new, but timeless. The pale blues and whites sweep across the ceiling making it resemble the sky. If you look at it for any length of time, you can see nymphs and beautiful faces peering down. The way the painting was done makes them muted, but it's as if they're there, watching down on you—and it doesn't matter if you notice or not—they're still there.

I tie my hair up into a loose bun on the top of my head, before grabbing my slippers from the bag. I lace up the ribbons of my pointe shoes around my ankles and stretch my muscles, bringing them to life.

I dance to the silent music playing in my head. I perform piqué turns over and over across the room, the world blurring around me. My lines are perfect, and everything is held in position, as it should be. Brisk grand allegros are counterbalanced by slow flowing adagios; all executed while keeping the utmost control over every muscle in my body. I'm holding myself in one piece instead of letting the fragments fall to the ground, finding inner and outer strength in my dancing.

Time becomes obsolete. I'm breathing hard, covered in sweat, my nightshirt clinging to my body like a second skin; it feels wonderful. I feel alive and ready to take on the world.

A rush of life courses through me as I dance in the center of the vast room. The shadows surround me, but they make no difference. If I hold focus, if I control the dance, then nothing can touch me here. Not Constance. Not Dad. No one.

I push my body to the edge. My muscles scream and my feet need attention, but the pain makes me feel alive. I know the burn of muscles and the sharp agony of pointe. I cause it, I control it, and I can stop it.

I'm breathing jaggedly now, and rush across the room with my arms out, bending forward, ready to go into another routine when I notice sapphire eyes watching me from the shadows. I stop abruptly and stifle a scream by pressing my fingers to my lips.

FROM MANGLED TOES TO BEARING ONE'S SOUL
November 2nd, 3:44am

Pete is sitting in a dark corner of the ballroom, straddling a chair, his front pressed against the backrest, one hand on his cheek. He makes no apologies. He simply says, "I love watching you dance. I can almost hear the music playing in my mind."

"Holy shit, Pete! How long have you been sitting there?"

"Long enough." He's utterly calm and it's completely aggravating.

"I'm not here to be your private peep show." I

turn without another word and sit on the floor to pull off my shoes. The knot on the ankle is tight so it takes me a moment. I hear Pete get up from his chair and pad toward me.

He picks up my bag, and places it next to me before sitting on the floor beside me. The air is charged like something weird is going to happen. I can't take more weird.

Pete runs his hand through his hair and stares at the wooden floor. "I've been here a while. I'm sorry I scared you, but I didn't want to interrupt and cause you to stop."

"Well, you should have. This was for me, I didn't want anyone to see." I undo the second knot on my other ankle and remove my second shoe. My eyes focus on my fingers, nervously wrapping and unwrapping the ribbon around them. Pete rests his hand on mine, gently stopping my fidgeting.

"I know." Pete presses his lips together and folds his hands in his lap before glancing over at me out of the corner of his eye. "I wish I could say I'm sorry, but I can't be sorry for watching you dance. You wouldn't have danced like that if you'd known I was here. It would have been muted, censored even. The way you dance when you think no one is watching is pure. It's like watching a poem coming to life. That wasn't only your body moving to music. You were baring your soul."

I cut him off, "Which is private."

"Some confessions can't stay private – they're too pure, too perfect."

I want to laugh but something tells me not to. "That was far from perfection, and unless you're studying to be my partner, you need to tell me what you're doing here. And don't make light of this and blow it off. You watching stole something honest from me. You owe me the same level of intimacy in return."

Pete doesn't laugh or blow it off. Instead, he remains next me and watches his hands. After a moment he takes a deep breath, nods in agreement, and parts his lips. "You're right. I owe you that."

I watch the side of his face out of the corner of my eye. My stomach flip flops in the moments of silence as I wonder what he's going to say. He could shatter this with a wry look or a joke, but he doesn't. The space is charged like there's lightning in the air, but it's all coming from him.

I reach for a little towel in my bag and pat my face. That's when he starts speaking again.

"It reminded me of me." He's tense but trying to hide it. He keeps the curve of his spine, but his eyes dart around the room as if he wants to run. Pete wrings his hands as he explains. "And I owe you more than a sentence since I saw something you didn't really want to share."

I glance at him. "No, I didn't—but I'm listening. Make us even Ferro. Tell me something that's connected to you on such a deep level, something you can share or show me, something you hide from the world."

He nods slowly and I can tell how hard it is for him to do this, but he does. He doesn't protest or tease me. "I don't know if this is enough, but it's not something I talk about. Ever. The books you found in my room—the poems. They're not just rhythmic words on paper. Poetry is a baring of the soul. It's making yourself vulnerable to the world with every word, every pang of pain, every tear of remorse. I see what I feel when you dance. I've been looking for a connection, wondering if they're similar—dancing and poetry. And I'm not certain, but both are beautifully strung together—forged by feeling, emotion, and technique—to form the perfect balance."

His words strip away my anger until I feel naked beside him. The way he speaks, with such conviction tempered with uncertainty—but a sincere desire to know—floors me. The words tumble out of my mouth because I can't hide my shock. "There's more? How can there be more?"

Did I just say that out loud? Eyes wide, I glance away from him quickly not wanting to fathom the expressions on his face. I'm in my damp nightshirt and panties, nothing else. I tuck my legs underneath me, trying to hide from him. But I feel naked regardless and what I just said made it worse.

Add in the fact that he saw me dancing and not some pre-arranged choreography that was meant to please an audience. He saw me pour every bottled up emotion I have onto the floor. The frantic desperation, the slow ticking of time, the melancholic sadness, the hopeful joy of something better yet to come. It's like he said, to the untrained eye, it's just movement, but Pete gets it, somehow.

"More? More, what?" His tone is so soft, so careful. Pete reaches for my hand and presses it lightly on top of mine. "Gina, tell me."

My stomach is swirling too fast. This is not supposed to happen. I can't think when he touches me. I slip my hand away from under his and look up into his intense sapphire eyes. "I can't. It's nothing." Fake smile, I find it and plaster it on my face before looking at him.

Pete's gaze sweeps over me before resting on my bare feet. They're mangled and less than pretty. "You know, there's no trace of anything like that in my life." He tips his head toward my feet.

I suddenly want to hide them and my face flushes with embarrassment. They're calloused, cracked, bleeding, and bandaged. They've been broken and repaired so many times that they don't look feminine any more. I try to laugh it off. "You mean a big ugly mess?" I smile at him.

For the first time in a long time, Pete meets my gaze and shakes his head. He swallows hard and confesses, "There's nothing ugly about your feet. They show passion, dedication, endurance, promise and hope. They are a testament to the type of person you are—you don't give up and you're willing to endure whatever it takes to get what you want, come Hell or high water." The corners of his lips rise for a moment and then fall. "I have nothing like that, and never will."

IT'S A DATE, DUDE!
November 2nd, 3:59am

His blue eyes study my face, and I wish he wasn't going to turn back into pumpkin Pete at daylight. I like this side of him, the way he's confident and vulnerable at the same time. He's honest with me and with himself. It's rare and I had no idea how deep these waters ran within him. That's why I blurted out there's more. I thought I knew the depths of him, but every time I think I've found the bottom, he goes deeper.

"I'm not so sure about that."

He looks up at me, hopeful and hesitant. "What do you mean by that?"

"I'm guessing you have books full of poems you wrote. You probably wrote them at all hours, through all things. I doubt the pages are pristine and perfectly white. They probably are smudged, written in emotional turmoil, and maybe some are stained with tears. Maybe." I smile at him carefully, quickly. "Writers tend to hide their hearts, don't they?"

He nods. "I suppose so."

The corner of my mouth pulls up.

"It seems dancers do the same thing—hide their hearts."

"Will you show me one day? One of your poems?" I try to catch his eye. Part of me thinks I shouldn't have asked, but the other part is jumping up and down like an 8-year-old on a trampoline.

Pete shakes his head and looks down to the floor, breaking all eye contact with me. His fingers toy with the frayed ends of satin at the tips of my shoes. "I never said I write poetry."

"Yes, you did. You said that—"

"No." His rebuttal is short and sharp, so unlike his earlier confessions. I should stop. I'm pushing his buttons, but I'm tired of this chasm between us.

"Why?" I demand, annoyed with him.

"Why what?"

"Why do you pretend to be someone you're not? Why do you deny that you write? So what if people know?"

"I have my reasons." His walls jut up, and form

turrets this time. I know I've lost the sentimental poet. For a brief moment, I had a friend in this empty, hollow house, but I'm back to being alone.

I rub my arms over my nightshirt, to ward off the sudden chill in the air. "I'm sorry I asked. You shared a personal moment with me, so I thought..."

He grins. "Yeah, personal for you maybe."

"You know what? Never mind." Hurt, I pick up my shoes and tie them together neatly. Once a fucking Ferro, always a fucking Ferro. Rules don't apply to them, or rather, they live by their own set of rules and, no matter who you are, there's no getting around it. It's only then that I notice Pete is still fully clothed, even though it's the middle of the night. "Why are you up at this hour, anyway?" I immediately regret asking. I don't want to know what he's been up to and, with his arrogant mask on, he'll be all too willing to describe his adventures in great, explicit detail. I toss my shoes into my dance bag and zip it up.

"Are you kidding?" Pete looks at me skeptically, then, when he sees my confused expression, continues in a gentle tone. "Gina, your room is across the hall from mine; I haven't had a decent night's sleep since you've arrived. Do you scream like that every night?"

Oh. My. God. My heart drops into my feet and I can't move. I can't breathe. "I don't want to talk about this."

"I understand. It's okay." Pete is quiet for a moment and he can tell I'm ready to bolt.

The thing is, I can't share that. Nightmares are so real and so terrifying. If he laughs and says it's nothing, I couldn't hold myself together anymore.

As if on cue, Pete says, "You don't trust me. I haven't given you reason to, it's just that—if I can do something…" He watches me standing there and gets up so he's in front of me. Pete catches my eye. "I will. You sound terrified and I can't help but feel it's my fault."

Damn it! I want to cry. I want to scream, throw my arms around his neck, and cry—but I do nothing. I just stand there and stare blankly. I refuse to speak because my voice will betray me. It's so late and I'm so tired. I can't do this anymore tonight. "I need to go to bed." I offer a weak smile and start to turn away.

Pete reaches for my arm, brushes his fingers against my elbow, but doesn't hold on. His hand drops back to his side, like he shouldn't touch me. "You don't have any weekend classes, do you?"

I look down at his hand and then back into his eyes. "No, I don't."

"All right then, I have an idea." Giving me a cocky grin, he bends down and lifts me up by the waist like I weigh no more than a feather. I yelp and squirm. His hold on my waist tickles. If I laugh, I'll wake up the entire mansion.

He sets me on my feet and looks down at me with a smug look of superior Ferro-ness. "Get to bed, Miss Granz, and try to get some sleep. Come and find me in the morning. I'm taking you out on a date."

"Me? On a date with *THE* Pete Ferro? That's kind of lowering my standards. I have a classy, wholesome image to maintain, you know, and associating with you might give people the wrong impression."

"I may have to duct tape that sassy mouth of yours shut one day. The way I see it, smartass, you're the one lowering my standards. I'm hot, and you're-" I put a finger to his lips, silencing him.

"If you value anything south of your belt, I suggest you not finish that sentence. I may be small, but I have pointy knees, and I'm not afraid to use them."

Pete removes my finger from his lips, kissing it lightly. "Temper, temper, Miss Granz. You didn't let me finish. I was going to say, *one cool chick.*"

We stand toe-to-toe, Pete looking down at me with mischief in his eyes, one eyebrow raised, waiting to see how I'll reply. He's giving me emotional whiplash, but I like his playful side.

"Listen, I appreciate your generosity, but you don't have to do this. I don't want your pity, and you have better things--er--hotter chicks to do. I'm actually tired of feeling like a thorn in your sexy side, so unless this is part of your mother's plan to give us more cuddly couple exposure in the public eye--"

He smirks. "You think I have a sexy side?"

I shake my head, smiling and gently beat him with my ballet slippers. Pete grabs my wrists on the second swing. "She'll probably have us followed by the media but no, this is not her idea, and I don't pity you. I'm actually kind of scared of you sometimes, especially when you're holding shoes."

"Really?" We laugh for a moment and I forget everything that's been bothering me. Pete is smiling fondly, revealing a dimple in his cheek. The dusting of stubble is heavier than usual and I have to resist the urge to touch his face and feel it under my palms.

"Go get some rest. I'll see you in the morning for our first date."

Pete walks into the hallway and turns the corner, heading toward his wing and our rooms. I steal a glance at one of the ornate floor-to-ceiling mirrors. For the first time since I've moved in, there's a smile on my face.

MY SORDID LOVE AFFAIR WITH A SLICE OF PIZZA

November 2nd, 12:02pm

Pete must read *Esquire* magazine, because damn—he looks completely edible in his black tight tee and perfectly worn jeans. That dark hair is casually combed, begging to be touched. The dusting of stubble on his chin is gone which makes me want to touch his face and slide my fingers over his smooth skin. When I get close to him, his scent hits me hard and I feel intoxicated. It's the perfect casual-not-trying combo to get laid. Maybe Pete writes articles for that magazine.

Add in his choice of transportation and I could

seriously swoon. We got here on his motorcycle. I love the rush that comes with the speed and wind in my face. Pete took the corners hard, leaning the bike further than I thought possible. I clung to his firm body, plastering myself against him and went with it. My heart raced the entire time and I couldn't stop laughing. Pete heard everything through the headset and I don't care. I'm not ashamed of letting other people see my emotions, not anymore. For the longest time I thought people would use them against me. Now my mantra has changed and can be summarized in two little words:

Fuck it.

Pete grabs my hand and pulls me across the street in the center, rushing across before another wave of vehicles plows us down. Horns blare around us as the city bakes in the afternoon sun. The light reflects off the glass windows and forms patches of shadow and light on the concrete. Steam billows up from a subway vent as he speeds down the sidewalk.

My guard is dropped. He's done nothing to make it return after last night. It's weird. This is the Pete that I thought existed, but I never thought I'd see him in daylight. It's like watching Dracula dancing in the sun in Times Square—it's weird and totally unimaginable—whether it's the real vampire or an actor prancing around in a cape. It's the kind of thing you have to see to totally understand. And here I am, seeing and believing. I was right. The other version of Pete is an echo compared to the man standing next me.

When my feet are planted firmly on the opposite curb, I laugh. "You lunatic."

Pete gives me that trademark look—that lopsided grin and glittering blue eyes—and teases, "I would have thought you'd like playing Frogger for real."

I choke on my laugh and it comes out like a snort. "Frogger! How old *are* you?"

Pete gets a bashful look on his face and glances at me out of the corner of his eye. He motions for me to follow him. "Sean was into vintage crap at one point. We had an Atari, Coleco, and the first version of Pong."

"Oh! Pong!" My voice is light, teasing.

Pete nods and shakes his head. "Can you even imagine Sean playing Pong?"

I think about it for a second and laugh. "Yeah, no. That's the biggest oxymoron ever. Badass Sean Ferro playing with his balls."

Pete stops in his tracks and raises a single brow while giving me an incredulous look. "Wow, so you have a thing for my brother's balls, do you?"

"Not his balls. Those are all dangly and hairy. Talk to me about the rest of him and this conversation will be a little bit different." I say it seriously because everyone knows his brother is hot—and crazy.

Pete watches my face for a second to see if there's anything there—anything I'm not telling him. "Sean is…I don't know. Sometimes I want to punch him in the face and make him wake up. Nightmares don't vanish on their own. You have to chase them off and make sure they don't come back."

He's referring to his brother's trial, but there's something in his eye, like he hopes I'll tell him why I wake up screaming every night. A chill runs down my spine thinking about the dreams, and the way they turn from soft images to burning horrors. My lips part, but I can't force the words out. For some reason, saying it out loud makes the nightmares seem more real. I laugh nervously and smile at the backs of my hands.

Pete reaches out and laces our fingers together. He can sense my distress, I know he can, which makes me even more skittish. I wonder what he'd do if I just took off down the street at a full run? That's the old Gina. I want to be brave and face whatever's next, but it feels like I ate a bucket of slugs.

Pete slightly drops his head to the side and catches my gaze. "Are you hungry? Because I know a great place—it's right over here."

I nod, thankful that he doesn't press me. "Yeah, sounds good."

Pete and I walk over to a restaurant. When we step inside, there's no one here. I pass over the threshold and stop, but Pete walks past me, beyond the podium and calls out, "*Roberto! Sei qui?*"

Holy crap. Pete speaks Italian. I'm not sure why I'm surprised, but I am. It rolls off his tongue like it's his first language. I blink away my shock and smile at him when he looks over his shoulder at me. A moment later a short, dark skinned man emerges from the back. He's wearing black slacks and a white button down shirt. His head is shiny like he was standing over a boiling pot. As soon as he sees Pete, he grins and throws open his arms. The stout guy gives Pete a bear hug and kisses his cheeks. Pete grins and the two converse in Italian for a moment with lots of smiles and back slapping.

Pete flips back to English. "Can you do it?"

Roberto nods. "*Si, si.*" He holds up a single finger in the air and darts away.

I cross the floor, moving around the empty tables, and head to the spot where Pete is standing. "Did you just ask him to open early for us?"

Pete looks like he might laugh. "No! Of course not."

"Then what'd you do?"

"Nothing!" He's close to laughing now, but I don't know why.

I poke my finger into his side and wiggle. Pete laughs and grabs my hands and turns me toward him. "I might have asked Rob to open today just for us. The man makes a killer pizza."

I blink at him. Then I look around. This isn't a

pizza parlor—not the greasy dollar slice kind of place. "You made him open for pizza?"

Pete presses a finger to the tip of my nose. "Yes, and when it's ready, you'll see why."

"Okay," I answer slowly, drawing out the second syllable.

Roberto appears a moment later with his black jacket complete with red carnation. He walks us to a back room that's bathed in candle light. The walls are different from the front. Instead of the dark wood, it's all white marble. The walls reach up about twenty feet high which is unusual for a restaurant here. A pale gold chandelier hangs above a small round table for two with posh white linens and fluffy chairs.

Roberto pulls out my seat. "*Signorina*."

I glance at Pete and then back at Roberto. They both smile, as if they know something I don't. I slip into my seat, and see a few more smiles before the man hurries away and I'm left alone with Pete.

He's sitting across from me, elbow on the table, and watching me with a goofy grin on his face. "You're going to love this."

I put my napkin on my lap. "I already do. How did you find this place?"

"Luck."

We chat for a little while as wine and antipasti are put on the table. I pick at the food, trying things that look familiar but different. After the plate is cleared Roberto appears with a silver serving tray held high above his head. He's grinning so wide that his ears are sticking out.

Pete's expression is similar. He looks as if he's about to jump out of his chair.

"*Per te.*" Roberto says as he places the tray in front of us. He beams as he slowly removes the lid to reveal the most beautiful piece of food I've ever seen.

Pete claps, twice loudly. "*Grazi*! It's beautiful! Gina, have you ever seen a better pie?"

I stare at it. This is man porn. It's an entire pizza pie that's fifty shades of gold. The golden crust has been brushed with it, the pepperoni have been draped in it, and the sauce—it's pale yellow. There are golden tomatoes mixed in with the yummiest looking cheeses ever. "Wow. Is that? Is it gold?"

Roberto is so proud he's ready to bust. Hands behind his back, he rocks up on his toes and explains. "23 karat gold leaf on the crust, Parisian cheeses, and Italian pepperoni. It's the Ferro specialty." He withdraws, still smiling as Pete grabs a slice and hands it to me on a white plate.

I start laughing. He looks up, worried. "What? Is this bad?"

"No, it's perfect. It's Peter Ferro, all grown up, but not. It's perfect, Pete. It really is. And if you tell me that you don't take any of your lady friends here, I may swoon on the spot."

He points a finger at me and says, "Don't mock me until you taste it. I don't do things half way."

"No kidding." Smiling, I lift the slice to my mouth and take a bite. The corners of my mouth drop instantly and I moan when the sauce, gold, bread, and cheese hit my tongue. I close my eyes for a second, and savor the taste.

When I look at Pete, he's watching me, leaning forward until his shirt lightly brushes against his slice of pizza. "That was worth watching. I should have recorded it."

I laugh and point at his shirt. "You have pizza on your man boobs."

"You orgasmed while eating pizza. It was worth it." He looks down and dabs the cheese and sauce off his shirt.

"I did not." I look at the slice and want another bite, but that cheese is so perfect and the sauce makes the flavors explode in my mouth. Add in the bling and it's too amazing for words.

"Go ahead. I won't judge." Pete grabs a slice and winks at me as he takes a bite.

"Fuck it."

"That's what she said."

Pete looks up at me from under his lashes with that crooked grin on his lips. I can't help it, I laugh.

Today has been unexpectedly wonderful.

FROM BIKER BOOTS TO DANCING SHOES

November 2nd, 3:28pm

Cars and yellow cabs pass by, honking incessantly. Tall skyscrapers surround us and throngs of people walk past as if they are all late for something. This city is always moving. It never stops.

If paparazzi are following us, they are very discreet about it, which is fine by me. Occasionally, Pete holds my hand, lacing our fingers together. I try to ignore the way it makes my stomach flip. I'm lonely and desperate for physical attention—even attention in the form of holding hands with a notorious womanizer and philanderer, even if it's only for the paps' much-needed pictures. I can't help but feel comfort with every little stroke of his thumb on the side of my hand.

As we pass a small secondhand store, something in the window catches my eye. I stop for a closer look. Pete hasn't noticed and keeps on walking. He's about two stores away, so I jog over to him and pull on his hand, stopping him.

"Hey, Pete? Do you remember at the merger gala when you asked me to teach you more swing dancing? Were you serious about that?"

Don't give the toothy smile, Gina. Act casual. I lace my fingers together and hold them in front of me, while I rock back on my heels slightly. Pete's brow rises as he steps towards me. The pit of my stomach goes into a free fall and the teeth try to come out. CHEESE. Damn it. Close your mouth! The result is horrendous. The corners of my lips tug up and twitch as if I had a hamster banging on my teeth and trying to escape from my mouth. Sexy!

Pete is a breath away, looking down at me. "Yes, I was serious. Why?"

I make a sound only dogs can hear as I pull Pete towards the store. Walking backward and holding onto both of his hands, I give him the full tooth grin. He follows hesitantly, eyebrows scrunched. It's the kind of store Pete wouldn't be caught dead in if not for the very insistent ballerina bossing him around.

"Come on then, big spender. We're getting you some dancing shoes."

I pull him into the shop, where we weave our way through a mix of secondhand and brand new merchandise. The air is thick with an undertone of moth balls and musty moisture. The scent takes some getting used to. I usher Pete to the back of the store and push him down onto the bench before I start rummaging through boxes.

A clerk helps us out and twenty minutes later, we step out of the store, shoe bag in hand and a smug look on my face.

"Now, lesson number one—biker boots are not dancing shoes."

Pete stops next to me, wraps an arm around my shoulders, and pulls me into his side. "You know why I agreed to this, right?"

I look up to him, grinning like a kid. "Because I have awesome taste, and you'll look fabulous in your new saddle shoes!"

Pete shakes his head. "Not quite. I agreed because the entire time we were in there, you had a loaded shoe in your hand. My face felt intimidated."

I bark out a loud laugh, making people stop and stare. I clap my hand over my mouth. We settled on a pair of black on black saddle shoes. Paired with a nice pair of tailored pants and button up shirt, he'll be even more scrumptious than he is now. I love his scruffy, battered up, bad boy look, but seeing him dressed in a tux knocked the wind out of me. That man can rock the formal look. I was tempted to get him the two-toned saddle shoes, black on white, to match my Oxfords, but he's not ready for that yet. Men have to ease into awesomeness. Maybe I'll get him spats and suspenders next.

Pete holds up the bag and looks at it before shaking his head. "Saddle shoes. My brothers are going to kick my ass after every other guy out there does."

"Men are so dense. Women love shoes and a guy in a hot pair of shoes is completely doable." I turn away, but Pete takes me by the hand and pulls me back toward him.

"Is that what this is about? Making me more doable? That might be hazardous to my health." Pete's chest brushes against mine when he laughs.

I lean in close, getting near enough to kiss him, but I don't. I tease, "It could be. The swagger, the tight shirts complete with beautiful biceps, let's not forget the aphrodisiac cologne, and now a pair of sexy saddle shoes." I tick off the items one by one on my fingers. "I don't know…maybe we should get you an insurance rider. It could be serious, women falling from the sky and landing on your dick might hurt. That could have unforeseen complications."

Pete moves quickly, pulls me against him and looks down into my eyes. He lingers there for a moment, until those crystal eyes are locked on my mouth. "You have a very dirty mouth, Gina Granz."

"Good thing you have all that soap, then." The pull between us is amazing. It reaches into every part of me, and it's becoming more difficult not to touch him. Fuck it. I press a finger to his lips and smile at him before ripping my body out of his force field of sexy vibes.

Pete remains perfectly still. It's as if he's stunned into silence. When he recovers, he takes my hand and we continue down the street.

IT'S ALL ABOUT CARPE'ING THE DIEM, DUDE!

November 2nd, 4:01pm

Pete is at a nearby bakery getting us freshly baked cookies and coffee. He's catering to my every whim, and I feel like a princess. While I wait for him to come back, I sit on the grass, in the middle of Central Park, watching people. It's early November. The air is chilly but not yet the finger numbing cold we get in the dead of winter. It's more like fluffy sweater weather. Luckily, I dressed warmly enough to enjoy the fresh, crisp air.

A gust of wind blows, tossing my hair every which way. Fallen leaves make their way across the lawn, spinning around like a dirt devil. One leaf falls onto my lap, and I pick it up. My hand crumples the dead foliage, sprinkling dried specks of brown on my shoes. Melancholy takes hold of me and squeezes tightly around my chest, making it hard to breathe. My eyes prickle and sting, but I hold back the tears. I pull my knees to my chest, wrapping my arms around my legs tightly.

Within the next couple of days, the trees will be completely bare, and the first snowfall will cover the ground, making everything look pure and white. Snow is supposed to bring the promise of happy times to come. Christmas lights, gift giving, and family gatherings.

But not this year, not for me.

My father is still treating me as if I don't exist. My mother and I barely see each other and getting out to see my friends is nearly impossible.

My thoughts get interrupted when Pete shows up, coffee tray in one hand and a paper bag in the other.

"I know you insisted, but they only had one macadamia nut cookie left. I hope that's okay? I got a ton of other snacks, too, since you randomly have the appetite of a caveman."

I beat my fists against my chest and make a grunting noise.

Pete laughs. "And that was?" Pete raises his cup of coffee to his lips and watches me from over the rim.

"My homo sapiens impression."

Pete spews and starts laugh-choking. He wipes his face with the back of his hand and sits down hard next to me, still chortling. "You are a homo sapiens! I think you mean Neanderthal."

I shrug and sip my coffee. "Same difference." I try not to smile and do a caveman voice. "Gina might need more science classes."

Pete laughs again, making his chest shake. "I can't tell if you're serious or if you're just screwing with me."

I reply in a silky, sexy voice, "A little of both." His eyes sweep over my face, as if he's just realizing there's more to know about me and he wants to dig deeper. I'm not sure what he's going to find because I haven't figured out what's in the basement of my soul yet. For all I know there's a whack-a-doo living down there. I might have to keep her chained up, so I divert his attention with a deadly serious topic. "Pete, I need to tell you something. There's a lot about me that you don't know, but this part is really important—don't eat my macadamia nut cookie."

The corner of his mouth pulls up. "I wouldn't dream of it. I made that mistake once. Never again."

I hold up my cup of coffee and Pete does the same. I tap them together. "Cheers. To health, happiness, gold pizza, and a truckload of cookies. Salute."

We sit in comfortable silence for a while, sipping our coffee, shoulder to shoulder. After a few minutes, I rest my head on his shoulder and sigh.

"What's the matter, G?" Pete's voice is soft, kind.

I don't want to spoil the day with my bipolar mood. "Nothing."

"I know it's something. You deflated when I went to get coffee, and that cookie should have perked you up. It didn't, so what's going on?" Pete doesn't look at me while he speaks so it doesn't feel like I have to answer, but I want to.

"It's nothing really. I was just thinking about the holidays and how I miss the way my family used to be—this year will be hard. Your family doesn't seem like a festive group. Somehow, I can't quite picture your mother singing carols or kissing anyone under the mistletoe."

I lift my chin up to catch Pete's reaction. His mouth quirks up to one side. "Yeah, not so much. They're more about grand ceremonies to flaunt the family's wealth. It has little to do with mirth or merriment."

Maybe Christmas won't be so bad if Pete can hold onto this nicer version of himself and can stick around long enough to spend some time with me. I swallow my sorrow and force a smile.

"Do you have any nice Christmas memories, Pete?"

"A few. Mostly from when we were kids--before we knew our family was a fucked up mess. Then it just became a tedious social event. You?"

"It used to be my favorite time of the year. My dad and I did this thing every year where he took me out for a special Father-Daughter date, a couple days before Christmas. We took in shows, sights, dinner, pictures with Santa, the tree at Rockefeller Center. When I was a little girl, Daddy told me that the Channel Garden Angels fly around the tree while we're sleeping, decorating it with magical snowflakes blown from their brass trumpets. It's the most efficient way to get lights up at the very top of the tree." The memory is bittersweet, but I shrug it off. Pete doesn't need to hear all that.

I pull out a fake smile and plaster it across my face. "But hey, things could be worse. I could be in a jail cell, sipping eggnog from my cellmate's bellybutton and trying not to comment on her I Heart Ponies tattoo."

Pete gags on his coffee. I look up to see he has a shocked expression on his face. "You're disturbing at times."

"It's a talent." I smile at him and then start thinking. "There is no way I would have imagined myself in this position. Ever. When I was a little girl, I did pretty much what all little girls do. I wished for the fairytale—the romantic courtship, bouquets of roses, the surprise engagement where the man drops to one knee with a diamond and a smile. Instead, I got a schedule, staged dates in front of reporters, and a betrothed whose little black book is bigger than the Bible. It's not a fairytale, but it's one helluva story regardless."

Pete sets his cup of coffee on the ground and pushes himself up. From the look of it, he's pissed. His shoulders are squared off, his hands closed into tight fists, his jaw clenching.

What the heck? I bare my soul and he's mad? "Pete?"

"I don't get you--sometimes you seem so fragile, but you always surprise me by getting back up each time life kicks you down. You have a temper that could easily rival my mother's, yet you forgive everyone around you. After everything you've been through, after having everything taken away from you, even after the way the people you love treated you, you still don't give up. Why? What's the fucking point?"

I hop up and grab his elbow, spinning him around. He looks down at me with those eyes and in that moment I swear I can see every thought, every emotion, and the war raging within him. "What am I supposed to do? Curl up into a ball and die? Screw that. I got a second chance, and I'm going to make sure I don't waste it, no matter what. On the night of that rave, I thought I was dead. Finished. Caput! There was no way for me to survive. My last thoughts before I passed out were about how I wasted my life. I had so many regrets, then you—of all people—saved me."

"Please don't glorify my actions from that night. You know why I did it."

"Yeah, yeah, I know you just wanted to bang a good girl. Stop interrupting me, Ferro, this is deep stuff and I don't share it too often."

Pete looks down at me from under his lashes. There's a softness to him that's usually hidden. "I don't know what to think—about anything anymore."

"Are you sure?" I step toward him, closing the space between us. I brush away a lock of hair that's hanging in his eyes and smooth it back. Tipping my head to the side, I rest my hand on his cheek. "I refuse to have any more regrets. If I cross a street today and get hit by a bus, I want to be able to say I did everything in my power to make my life awesome. I can't do that if I give up. It's not for nothing, Pete. Life isn't a sick joke with no point."

"You can't make past regrets vanish. What's done is done and will follow us to our graves no matter what we do."

My hand falls to my side as a somber wave of regret washes over me. "We're both changing, I can feel it. It's frightening because we don't know where we'll end up, and I don't mean a prison cell versus a mansion—it's more than that. I can't change what happened, I can't erase the mistakes I've made. I can't make my father forgive me, and I don't get the fairytale with the white knight. Instead, I've been given other things. A friend came out of that fire. I don't know about you, but I really needed one then—someone who understood having a tyrannical parent and being an utter disappointment. For some reason, the two of us, in our failings gives me strength. I found hope again and I'm not living my life looking backwards. I'm grateful for what I have now, right this second."

I press the pad of a finger to his nose. Pete doesn't move. His gaze remains fixed on the yellowing grass. He inhales slowly before speaking. "Me? You're grateful for me?" He asks the question as if it's a cruel joke.

My eyes sting and it's everything I can do to hide it. I throw my arm around his shoulder and tug him against me. Since I'm short, it doesn't work very well. Actually, it's silly—which is what I hoped for. "I am. This ballerina really jives with your inner poet. You should let that mofo out more often."

Pete laughs unexpectedly and turns toward me. "Maybe I will."

COOKIES, KISSES, AND CROWS

November 2nd, 4:28pm

Pete flops down onto the grass, lying on his back, and stares at the sky. He seems lost in thought. We stay silent for a long time. After a little while, he pulls me to him, and I use his chest as a pillow. I'm in a daze, in that comfortable spot between wake and sleep. The steady beating of his heart lulls me into a relaxed contentment.

He shifts slightly under me, and I vaguely distinguish the sound of a paper bag being crumpled. He moans once, the way I did eating the gold pizza earlier. He moans again, but this time it almost sounds erotic. My mind drifts in and out, and I'm not quite sure if I'm dreaming or if Pete Ferro is actually moaning under me.

"This, is amazing" he says, his voice husky and heavy.

"Uh-huh," I breathe.

"No, really, Gina, this cookie is amazing. I'm so glad you were willing to share it with me. No wonder you love these—they're orgasmic."

Uh... I open my eyes and push myself up. He's eating my macadamia nut cookie. It's the only one in the bag, and now it's stuck between Pete's perfect lips. His crooked smirk is back, along with that damned dimple, and a sparkle in his beautiful eyes.

I reach down to grab it from his mouth, but one of his hands grabs my wrist, firmly. "Don't. You. Dare."

He waggles his eyebrows.

I reach again with my other hand, but he catches my wrist. My body twists to the side, both wrists clasped in his grasp, and I try to wriggle my way free, but it's useless. I don't have a choice. If I want that cookie, I have to do it the sexy way.

I dip my head down, and my teeth grab hold of the cookie. I pull up, but the cookie won't budge. He's not letting it go. I bite off a chunk and straighten up. I make an erotic sound in the back of my throat as I swallow the bite.

I glance down with a victorious grin but falter.

There's still too much of that cookie trapped in between his lips, and I want more, so much more. I shift, to straddle his hips, and sit just below his stomach. Pete's eyes widen in surprise, but he doesn't say anything because his mouth is occupied with the remainder of my cookie.

"You know, I kind of like that you can't talk right now, Ferro. Makes you a lot more attractive. I think I may get you a gag for Christmas or maybe as a wedding gift. I wonder if they sell cookie gags."

His lips quirk up and somehow, he manages to make the cookie drop further into his mouth, slowly disappearing just a little at a time.

"Oh, no you didn't!"

His only response is to waggle his eyebrows cockily. I'll have to wax those suckers off of him one night while he's sleeping. I can see it now: undercover Jenny tiptoeing through Ferro mansion, hot wax in hand. She reaches Pete's rooms and finds him sleeping in bed.

Back to matters at hand—I want that cookie.

The next move will be tricky. There's no way I'll be able to retrieve the remaining bite without touching his lips at least a little bit, like a kiss. Like a meaningless stage kiss, only it's not a kiss. Nope. Not a kiss. It's a sly ninja move to save my macadamia nut goodness from the evil jaws of sexy death.

It's a rescue mission. Save the cookies!

Yes, I can do this!

I look into Pete's eyes and completely lose my nerve when massive knots start to form in the pit of my stomach. I can't kiss him, not even a little bit. I'm over thinking it and it feels like I'm standing at the edge of a cold swimming pool, dreading to put my big toe in, fearing the cold sting. The longer I stall, the more I lose my courage.

Pete makes the decision for me. He tugs on my wrists and pulls me down toward him. It's all about the cookie, Gina. It's not about his lips. I'll just take that last little bite and back off as quickly as I can. I part my lips and wrap them around the cookie. They gently touch his in a sweeping motion. He pushes the last little piece of the cookie into my mouth with his tongue, softly caressing my bottom lip in the process. Liquid heat shoots through every single cell in my body, and I gasp. I try to back away, but Pete keeps me close. His eyelids drop, and he starts kissing me lightly.

His kiss is tender and perfect, and I struggle to remember that this is his MO, his specialty. He's the master player, making women swoon with a smile and a meticulously perfected kiss. I try not to kiss him back but, with the chewing and the swallowing, he thinks I'm returning it. He lets out a sigh, and his tongue strokes my bottom lip once more.

It breaks me. I can't hold off any longer.

With the cookie long gone, I kiss him back,

opening myself to him, and welcoming his kiss. I forget everything but the feel of his soft lips and the taste of his tongue as it dances with mine. I melt into him, and he places my hands on his shoulders before letting go of my wrists. With one hand, he cradles my head, twisting my hair in between his fingers, while his other hand goes to my back, pressing me firmly against him.

God, I've missed this. I've missed him. The first time Pete kissed me, it felt like my first time, like I'd never been kissed before. This, right here, feels like coming home. Pete's hands travel everywhere at once, down my shoulders, along my back. I feel safe once more in his embrace, which is exactly why I have alarms and bells clanging loudly in my head, telling me to stop this. I ignore them. It's like being in the eye of a storm. Complete calm amidst the destructive chaos around me. I know that this will destroy me, but I let it happen because I'm too weak to stop it. I need it. I crave it.

I'm lost in his lips, and I don't want it to end. His mouth breaks away from mine as he lightly brushes kisses over my cheekbones, down my jaw, delicately caressing every part of my face. Our eyes meet briefly and something snaps. All tenderness is gone and replaced by something else, something all consuming. Our lips meet again in a deeper, more passionate connection where every sweep of his tongue against mine sends me into a whirlwind of sensual hopefulness. My body aches for him. His hands keep me close the entire time, as if afraid I might run away. My fingers play with his hair, tugging every once in a while, earning a couple of the sexiest groans I've ever heard to reverberate in my mouth. He grasps my hips and squeezes, pressing me down at the same time as he pushes his hips upwards. I gasp. The pressure feels so good. He hits that sweet spot down below, and I rock into him once.

"Oh, God! More." I moan shamelessly into his mouth, and he gives me more.

He presses his hips to mine again, growling my name into the kiss.

His hands travel up my body until they cup my face, allowing Pete to sever our connection gently. We're not just breathless; we're both panting. I press my forehead against his and try to catch my breath. Pete's face breaks into a lazy smile, his eyes still closed. His eyelashes flutter as if he's slowly waking up from a deep sleep. He is truly beautiful beyond compare, like a sexy angel that fell from the sky.

Pete looks at peace, and I trace every perfect feature with the pads of my fingers. He turns his head to the side and opens his eyes. "There, that should do the trick, don't you think?"

"Huh?"

"Over there." He nudges with his chin. "Paparazzi. Hopefully, this will appease my mother, and she can get off your back for a while." Pete points to a bush where photographers shoot in our direction.

My heart beats once and then plummets so far, so fast that it makes me gasp for air. It was all an act? Damn it! Of course, why else would he kiss me like that?

Constance had us followed; Pete saw the photographers hiding, and he gave them what they wanted. It's as simple as that, just like when he was holding my hands earlier. I knew this wasn't real, not for him. It's not like it was real for me, either. We're friends. That's all we are, and all we'll ever be.

"Good plan." I force a plastic smile on my lips and hide everything else. "Thanks." I push myself up, wanting some distance, but Pete holds me there, grasping my hips and pulling me down on his--disco stick!

"Wait, don't move!" he says. I try to wriggle free but, he's holding me too tightly.

"Relax, Pete. You can let me go. You're wearing jeans. No one will see your ginormous boner." Pete's mirth filled eyes connect with mine. "Ginormous, huh? It's nice of you to notice, but that's not what I meant." He reaches for the paper bag next to us, takes another cookie and, before placing it in between his lips again, says, "Ready for round two?"

My brow lifts slightly as my lips part. What? Do I want to do this again? The kiss was perfect, but I feel like I'm drowning in lust and things that will never be. But those lips, and deep blue eyes.

I suck in air suddenly, not realizing that I stopped breathing.

My eyes dart to the side. No, I'm not ready for round two. Every time we kiss, it results in him taking a piece of my heart. I don't know how many times I can do this before there's nothing left. I have to keep him in the friend zone. I can't do the casual, flirtatious kisses without any true feelings behind them, not with Pete. Still, I don't want him to know what he does to me.

My mask is on, and my walls are up. I smirk at him and push off his lap in a playful way that nearly brushes a nipple across his cheek. I'm a tease in that moment, I'm someone else—someone who doesn't care.

"Sorry, Pete. I don't do chocolate chip. I'm not that kind of girl. I told you I was classy."

I'm crouched in Pete's face, ready to straighten when a couple of black crows whip past me. One pelts me in the head. I startle and fall onto Pete's lap. I'm trapped by Pete's thighs propped up behind me.

At the same time, Pete starts to thrash. The crows are swarming and pecking at his face. I let out a scream.

"Omigod! Omigod! Omigod!" I flap my hands like I'm one of the birds. The crows keep pecking away at Pete's face and his arms flail like mad, trying to get the birds away.

Pete is mumbling something. He can't talk because his mouth is full of cookie and crows. It sounds like "Gnff! Gnff!" It takes a minute, but then I put it together.

Oh, shit! He's saying, *get off!*

I manage to roll onto the grass, and Pete stands up, swatting the birds away. But the crows don't leave. They stick around, pecking at the remains of the chocolate chip cookie Pete spat on the ground. The look on his face is priceless. I've seen Pete fight. I've even seen him up close when he has that angry look in his eyes, but nothing comes close to the venom he's giving those crows.

I crawl over to the birds, shooing them away before he can commit birdicide. They take flight and Pete jumps, covering his head with his arms. It's too much. I roll on the ground, laughing my ass off.

"Oh, my God! Pete Ferro! Scared of little birds! Tweet, tweet!" I howl in between laughs.

Pete doesn't think it's funny. He picks up our things, helps me up roughly and stomps off, pouting.

"Aw, Pete! Come back! They just wanted some of your loving too! Come on! Give a bird a cookie!" Pete flashes the middle finger at me, walking away in a huff. I have to run to catch up with him.

Every time a bird flies by, Pete jumps and covers his head, making me laugh even harder.

A SMIDGEN OF CATNIP
November 16th, 9:19am

I stare at my phone's screen, sitting cross-legged on my bed, surrounded by open notebooks. How did my love life get so complicated?

I read Philip's text message over and over again as if I'll see the answers if I just read it one more time.

I'm sorry I got angry. I miss you. Please meet me at the club tonight? I want us to work this out, somehow. I need to see you

It's been two weeks since my date with Pete. I haven't seen or heard from him since, except hearing his door slam when he comes home in the middle of the night and when he leaves early in the morning. I have no clue where he goes or what he does, and I'm not in any hurry to find out. Even the gossip rags and newspapers haven't mentioned anything about him lately.

Apart from our heated kiss in Central Park, I feel like I'm closing in on nunnery more and more every day. I think back on my talk with Pete, the one about having no regrets. I don't want to be unloved and untouched forever. Philip's invitation is tempting. I hate that we parted on such bad terms, and we did have a connection. He knows about Pete now, yet he still wants to see me and patch things up. Maybe I should give this a try.

The intercom buzzes and the butler's voice rings throughout my room. "Miss Granz, there's a Mister Anthony Cleary at the door for you. He seems to be inebriated. Should I let him in or escort him off the premises?"

Anthony? What is this, revenge of the exes? What the hell? I haven't heard from him since my betrothal to Pete, and I have nothing to say to him. I am curious though why he's here and inebriated this early in the morning--that's so unlike him.

I get up and walk to the intercom on the wall and click on the button. "I'll be down to see him in the grand foyer, but you're staying close, just in case. Thank you."

"Very good, ma'am," he replies, and I hear the

intercom click off.

I quickly key in a reply to Philip's text, drop the phone on the bed and head towards the mirror. My hair is a mess because that's what studying for finals does to my 'fro. I secure my hair on top of my head with a bandana and grab a sweater before I head out of my room. The heels of my oxfords click on the cold marble tiles.

Though my surroundings have become familiar, this place still feels cold and unwelcoming. My nightmares don't help ease that feeling. I'm still waking up, out of breath, having sprinted down the frost covered halls of the Ferro mansion every night.

I make it to the top of the stairs and see Anthony pacing by the large wooden door in the grand foyer. The butler stands close by, keeping a non-threatening distance, hands clasped behind his back.

I clear my throat and make my way down the spiraling steps. Anthony sees me and runs toward the bottom of the stairs. The butler twitches, but I nod to him to stay where he is. Anthony isn't a threat. He's never passionate or brash about anything. He's the human equivalent of porridge. Baby bear's porridge. Not too cold, not too hot, just plain, boring, lukewarm porridge, with a smidgen of catnip. What did I ever see in him?

He looks awful. His hair is dirty and much too long, his face is unshaven, his eyes are bloodshot, and his clothes look like he's been sleeping in a dumpster for the past week. And the smell! Drown a dead rat in beer, and let him stew in the sun for a day, and you still wouldn't get close to the stench wafting off of Anthony.

"Anthony?" I reach the bottom of the steps and cross the foyer toward him. This is not like him at all. He was always exceptionally clean, preppy, and put together. The man before me doesn't match the person I used to know at all.

"Regina, it's you!" He exhales my name as if I'm a mirage. I have to put my hands over my mouth and nose to block out the stench. Anthony holds out a filthy hand towards me, but I take a small step back. The butler moves in a bit closer, but not enough to be intimidating. Anthony sees that his every move is being watched and lowers his hand, backing away from me.

"What are you doing here and what happened to you?" He was a dick, but I can't help but feel empathy for the broken man in front of me.

"I was told you live here now. I needed to talk to you. I don't understand what happened, baby. I was hoping you could tell me. One moment we're engaged, and I'm on my way to becoming a doctor, working for your dad, and being the luckiest shit on the planet. The next moment, I'm being served legal documents explaining the end of our engagement and how I'm to stay away from you. I was told if I tried to contact you, I'd get hit with a restraining order. Your father fired me, and the school took away my Granz scholarship. I can't pay for med school, Regina. I was so close! My work is done, but they won't give me my diploma because I still owe them money."

The more Anthony talks, the more I feel myself unraveling, guilt pulling me down again. I thought I fixed everything by accepting Constance's offer, but in solving my problem, I've caused one for Anthony. I've done this to him.

No, he did this to himself, Gina. Stop taking the blame for everything.

The new me tries to take a stand, determined to push through and fight for herself, instead of being walked on and used. I let her take over. "Anthony, we were never engaged. You never proposed. You cheated on me the day before my father ordered me to marry you and had no qualms living with a lie or marrying me under false pretenses. You only wanted to pretend we were fine because it was to your advantage. You used and deceived me. I'm sorry for your financial situation, but I wouldn't help you even if I could."

"Is that what this is about, Regina? Dammit, it was just sex! It didn't mean anything. I love you, and that means everything! I'm sorry I cheated on you, okay? I was confused and under a lot of stress. It was stupid, and I won't ever do that to you again. Is that what you want me to say? How can I make it up to you? Please take me back! You have to take me back!" He's begging, desperate to regain his former life.

My hand grips the iron railing tightly enough to hurt, but my words are soft and controlled. "You never loved me. You hardly even cared for me. You didn't even want to touch me, Anthony. Do you know how much that hurt? How much it still hurts? You wanted my money and my connections so badly you forced yourself to share a bed with me. You weren't in love with me, you were repulsed by me, and now I'm repulsed by you. I won't take you back, not now or ever. Goodbye, Anthony."

I nod to the Ferros' butler, a silent request for him to escort Anthony out. I turn around to climb the steps to my room. I don't want him to see my unshed tears; I don't want him to think they're for him. They aren't. Months of rejection have taken their toll, and I yearn to have someone who wants me for a change.

Suddenly, I feel a firm hand on my shoulder, pulling me back. "No! You have to take me back." Anthony's voice is desperate. The pain in his voice is too much. I can't crush another human being's spirit.

I want to answer him kindly, tell him it's not too late for him to turn his life around, but his hand is ripped away from my shoulder before I get a chance to speak.

"Get your fucking hands off of her, you worthless lowlife piece of shit!"

That voice. That angry, hate-filled voice echoes, booming around the grand foyer, promising nothing but pain and bloodshed.

UH-OH!
November 16th, 9:40am

Pete stands menacingly behind Anthony, holding onto him by the shoulder. He's shirtless, and the top button of his jeans is undone. Pete's body language screams one word: fight. His muscles cord tightly, every tendon tensing as he clenches and unclenches his fist.

My hands lift, like I could stop him. I have to stop him. "Pete, no. Let him go."

Pete doesn't acknowledge me. The two men face each other, competing in an instinctual glaring contest. Anthony doesn't stand a chance in this fight, and it scares me. He's having trouble focusing his eyes on anything as it is, and he can barely stand without wobbling. He's not physically strong sober, much less shit-faced drunk.

Anthony blinks a couple of times and stabs a finger at Pete's chest. "Hey. Aren't you that Ferro guy who was nailing all the girls at Regina's house? Man, you gotta let me know what your secret is! I could definitely use that kind of pussy act--"

Pete's fist connects with Anthony's jaw before Anthony can finish his sentence. Anthony loses his footing and stumbles backward but doesn't fall. I let out a scream and hold onto the cold railing with both hands.

"Stop it, Pete. Please!" Pete continues to ignore me. The butler stands still, letting the fight take place. The future master of the house is in no danger, so there's no need to intervene.

Anthony shakes his head in confusion and rubs his jaw. "What the hell, man?" Anthony looks at me, dazed, and then at Pete and back to me.

He raises a single finger in a drunken Eureka moment. "Wait a minute. I get it. Regina, you're one of Ferro's tramps now, aren't you? Is that what this is about?" He turns to Pete and puts both hands up in the air. "Hey, man. I won't prevent you from nailing her, if that's the hangup." He puts his hand up to his face thinking that he's keeping the conversation secret from me, but he's talking loud enough that the household staff watching from the main landing above can still hear. "Are you sure you want her, though? I mean it's just Regina. It's not like she's a good lay or anything. Trust me."

Those words pierce me through to my core. To have Ferro mansion staff witness this is embarrassing, but to have Pete hear it, is excruciating. My lips part and I can't hide the way my lower lip trembles. I snap it shut, trying to hide my pain, but it's too late.

Pete grabs Anthony by the shoulder and lands a punch in his stomach, making me jump.

"You shut the fuck up about Gina."

"Anthony, please, just leave." My voice is trembling and weak. My hands hold onto the railing so hard that they are starting to hurt. I want him gone before any more damage can occur, but Pete doesn't stop his assault. He doesn't let Anthony reply or give him the chance to leave. He's lost all self-control. He pushes Anthony up against a wall and punches him over and over again, holding him up with his other hand.

His fist connects with Anthony's face. A sickeningly loud crunch makes my stomach roil. It's the sound of bones breaking, and I scream, but no one listens. Pete lets Anthony fall to the ground on his knees, blood pouring out of his very crooked nose. His movements are slow and sluggish. He brings his hands to his face, not even trying to protect himself. Pete moves in and kicks him in the stomach. Anthony doubles over and falls onto the floor.

Oh, my God! He's going to kill him if he doesn't stop. I run down the stairs and throw myself between them. "STOP!"

I'm stuck in between Pete's fury and his target, a sense of déjà vu taking over. I place my hands over his fist and look him straight in the eyes. "Please. Stop."

Pete's gaze darts from me to Anthony.

Chest heaving and his skin covered with a fine sheen of sweat, Pete drops his fist. "Move, Gina, and let me take care of this motherfucker. I saw what he did to you. I was there that night."

"No, I won't move. And I was there too, remember?"

"Why are you protecting him?" Pete is yelling, pointing towards Anthony who is slouched against the wall behind me.

"I'm not." I blink back tears and try to keep my voice low and calm. "I'm not protecting him. I couldn't care less about him. I'm protecting *you*." I try to swallow but my throat has a lump in it that won't move.

Pete's face contorts. It's as if I insulted him. "That's ridiculous. I can take on five guys like him, all at once."

Inhaling slowly, I let the air fill me up and calm me down. This isn't the time to be cautious, but I can't help it. It feels like my heart was trampled. I want to shove the remains in a box and retreat to my room, but I can't. I can't let Pete do this to himself. He doesn't even see it.

I press my lips together for a moment and find the right words. "I know you can, Peter. You are a badass fighter, but that's not what I meant."

Whoops and hollers echo around the vast room. I turn around to see young Jonathan swinging himself over the banister of the stairs and landing a couple feet away from us, shirt unbuttoned and flying behind him like a superhero cape. "Hell yeah! Finally, some action in this house."

"Leave, Johnny," Pete scolds his younger brother, warning him off. "This doesn't concern you."

Jonathan's face drops just a fraction of a second. I wouldn't have recognized it if it weren't for the fact that I've become accustomed to that feeling. It was there for the briefest of moments--hurt, rejection, loneliness. On Jonathan, the look is quickly replaced by amusement at the prospect of getting into some kind of trouble.

The butler moves in and takes hold of Anthony, restraining his arms tightly behind his back. Anthony doesn't fight back. "What should I do about our guest, Miss Granz?"

I glance from seething Pete, to battered Anthony, to hopeful Jonathan. "Jonathan, could you please escort Anthony off the premises?"

"Sure thing," he says, his face lighting up. "Anything for you, gorgeous." Jon winks at me and grabs hold of Anthony's elbow, leading him toward the front door. "C'mon! It's garbage day," he says a bit too happily. "Don't want to miss your ride out of here, do you, buddy?"

I take hold of Pete's hand and pull gently. I don't need to say anything more, he just follows.

"Regina! Please don't do this," Anthony protests on his way out the door. "I didn't mean it! I love you, Regina! You're making a huge mistake." Anthony's voice becomes an echo the further away we move from the foyer. I lead Pete towards the ballroom and close the massive double doors behind us, shutting everyone else out.

Pete paces the floor. He's blowing off steam, hands busy ruffling his hair and nostrils flaring as he tries to get his breathing under control.

I push myself off the door and make my way in front of him, interrupting his pacing. I place a hand on his cheek, and he closes his eyes, leaning into my touch. His shoulders eventually drop, and his back isn't quite so stiff.

"Peter?" His eyes open and they are noticeably calmer than even a few moments ago. "This needs to stop. Fighting like this—it's destroying you. I see a good man in front of me, someone I care about, and someone who's fiercely passionate and willing to go to great lengths to protect me. As your friend, I'm begging you to stop. If not for you, then do it for me."

"Gina, I…"

I take both of his lips in between my fingers and pinch them shut to shush him. He'll probably bite me, but I don't care, I don't let him talk. If I do, he'll come up with dumb excuses.

"No, let me talk. Remember when I told you about going through life without regrets and to make every moment count?" Pete looks away, avoiding my gaze, but I pull on his lips, forcing him to look at me. "It's time for you to make some changes. You spend all your time screwing women, getting into nasty fights, and spending your money on crap. That's not living. Your words are so powerful, and they can build faster than your fists can destroy. There are worlds inside of you, aching to get out. There are things you could do, because of who you are and I don't mean your name. Being a Ferro only takes you so far. There's something else that's more powerful laying beneath the surface and you hardly ever tap into it. That man is amazing."

Pete gently removes my finger clamp from his mouth and watches me uncertainly. "It's not that simple."

"I never said it was easy," I reply, folding my arms across my chest and cocking my head to the side. "In fact, it's harder to channel all that rage into something else, but you have to do it. This path you're on won't end well, Peter. And you have so much more to offer. All I'm saying is you need to find an outlet for all the pent-up rage and passion you have locked up in here." I place a hand on his bare chest. His skin is hot and soft; his heartbeat is steady and strong.

Pete places a hand over mine, over his heart and moves in closer. There's only an inch in between us. He looks down at me and lifts my chin with his other hand. "What do you suggest?"

"Do something that's worthwhile with that raw emotion. It's dying to come out, so channel it. Grab hold and realize that you're attempting to grab lightning. It'll be hard and it may hurt, but my God, Peter—you could do so much besides smash things."

"It sounds like you see something that's not there."

"Bullshit. I see exactly what's there. Potential that's been locked away and banished from sight. Maybe that guy scares you, but he doesn't frighten me. Very few people have been given such gifts, and the means to use them. Use that passion that's locked up inside of you and do something beautiful with it." I look down to the ground and then look up at him, smiling shyly. "Something like this..."

BALLROOM BITCH
November 16th, 10:06am

I place my hands on Pete's waist and move in slowly. My hands slide against slick skin, from his waist to his back, slowly traveling toward the rear pockets of his jeans. Pete's eyes widen with confusion. It's a struggle not to focus on how firm and perfect his butt is under my fingertips, or how close his bare chest is to my face, or the enticing scent that is unique to him. Pete's breathing accelerates, and I feel him tense up, anticipating my next move, but that's not what this is about--this is about one friend helping another.

I try to repress the mixed feelings brought on as

my fingers make out the distinctive shape of a condom packet in one of his pockets, pushing that thought aside to ponder later. I wrap my fingers around the prize and take a step back, handing him his phone.

"Music, maestro?"

Pete's expression softens with understanding and, after a few taps and swipes of his fingers across the screen, Duke Ellington's music plays with pure clarity over the ballroom's expensive surround sound system. It feels as if there's a brass band playing all around us. He tucks the phone back in his rear pocket, smiles, and takes my hands, planting a kiss in each palm.

"Thank you, Gina, for everything." His smile is soft and genuine, no trace of arrogance or anger left.

"You're welcome, Peter. Now, I want you to make me fly. There are a couple gnarly throws I'm dying to show you."

We warm up with basic rock steps, lindy hop steps, and simple spins, smiling and laughing as we do so. I let him lead for now because, let's face it, he's an excellent dance partner, and being led by Peter Ferro is quite the thrill. His moves are sure, confident and playful, his hands are possessive and, for the briefest of moments, I feel like I'm truly his.

I let go of his hands and stop dancing, slightly out of breath. "Ok, so I want to try a new move with you. What you're going to do is..."

My explanation gets interrupted when a short, petite woman with long brown hair comes barging into the ballroom, shoulders bare, covered only by a bedsheet wrapped around her body. Pete doesn't notice her at first. His back is to the door, but I get a full view of the pretty woman standing in front of me. She has that natural beauty that'll make most women scream. Case in point, she's wearing nothing but a bed sheet and looks fabulous.

"Here you are!" She says in an airy voice. "I've been looking everywhere for you. When are you coming back to bed? I'm getting lonely."

Pieces snap together. His bare chest, top jean button undone, condom in his rear pocket, the naked girl calling him back to bed.

He brought a woman home last night.

Peter never brings women home. I had been the exception, until now.

He broke his single rule.

This woman is not some random floozie. She's someone special. That's why he's been gone for the past two weeks and hasn't made the news once. I thought he was respecting my limits and keeping his conquests out of sight out of respect for me. But that's not it. He was away, being happy with her. My eyes sting, not certain if it's from sadness or anger. The last little shred of self-esteem I had left snaps.

Pete's eyes shift between the woman and me, looking dumbfounded. He opens his mouth to talk, but doesn't get a chance to. My hand flies and slaps him hard across the face. I wince and grab my hand. Fuck. That. Hurts!

My heart shatters as I realize Pete might genuinely care for someone else.

I need to get out of here. My heart and my head are screaming things at me, things I don't want to hear. Things I don't want to acknowledge. Because if I do, everything changes. I don't give Pete time to react, before I run, hand throbbing, pushing my way past the woman and out into the hall. My last thought that registers, before I leave them behind, is that she smells like sex.

"Gina!" Pete calls to me, but I don't stop.

I have no clue where I'm running to, but I cut corners to try and lose him. He's faster than me and will catch up in no time. I need to get away from here.

"Gina, let me explain!" His voice is getting closer.

I need to hide somewhere. I don't want to hear his explanations. I can't take any more lashes, and my heart is completely broken. Being sidelined because the man is incapable of anything except meaningless fucks hurts; being sidelined because the man I love has fallen for someone else is excruciating. I gasp, unable to breathe as realization finally catches up with me.

Panicked, I open the first door I see and silently

slip my way into the room, closing the door behind me. I collapse on the floor, my back pressed up against the hardwood door. This can't be happening.

I love Peter Ferro.

COMING SOON:

LIFE BEFORE DAMAGED
Volume 9
THE FERRO FAMILY

*****

To ensure you don't miss H.M. Ward's next book,
text AWESOMEBOOKS (one word) to 22828
and you will get an email reminder on release day.
*****

Want to talk to other fans?
Go to Facebook and join the discussion!

COVER REVEAL:

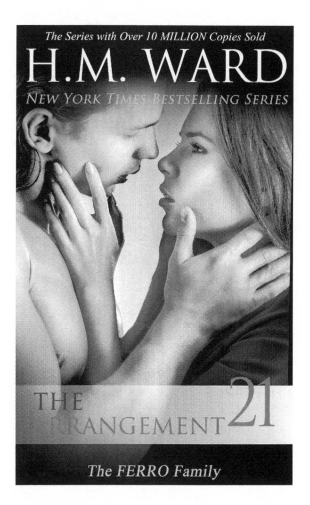

The Series with Over 10 MILLION Copies Sold

H.M. WARD

NEW YORK TIMES BESTSELLING SERIES

THE ARRANGEMENT 21

The FERRO Family

MORE FERRO FAMILY BOOKS

NICK FERRO
~THE WEDDING CONTRACT~
*****

BRYAN FERRO
~THE PROPOSITION~
*****

SEAN FERRO
~THE ARRANGEMENT~
******

PETER FERRO GRANZ
~DAMAGED~
******

JONATHAN FERRO
~STRIPPED~
******

MORE ROMANCE BY H.M. WARD

SCANDALOUS

SCANDALOUS 2

SECRETS

THE SECRET LIFE OF TRYSTAN SCOTT

DEMON KISSED

CHRISTMAS KISSES

SECOND CHANCES

And more.

To see a full book list, please visit:
www.sexyawesomebooks.com/#!/BOOKS

CAN'T WAIT FOR H.M. WARD'S NEXT STEAMY BOOK?

⭐⭐⭐⭐⭐

Let her know by leaving stars and telling her what you liked about
LIFE BEFORE DAMAGED, VOL. 8
in a review!

COVER REVEAL:

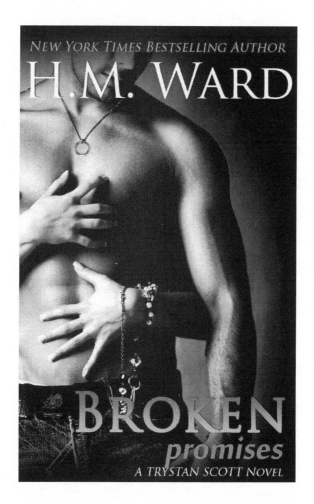

NEW YORK TIMES BESTSELLING AUTHOR

H.M. WARD

BROKEN
promises

A TRYSTAN SCOTT NOVEL

56644333R00072

Made in the USA
Lexington, KY
26 October 2016